JUST PLAIN
FANCY

To Justine Marie Arvold
and the plain fancy miracle
that brought her to us

JUST PLAIN FANCY
A Bantam Little Rooster Book / October 1990

Little Rooster is a trademark of Bantam Books, a division of Bantam Doubleday Dell
Publishing Group, Inc.

Published by Bantam Books, a division of Bantam Doubleday Dell Publishing Group, Inc.
Published simultaneously in the United States and Canada.
Printed in Hong Kong by South China Printing Company (1988) Limited

Library of Congress Cataloging-in-Publication Data

Polacco, Patrica.
    Just plain fancy / by Patricia Polacco.
        p. cm.
    Summary: Naomi, an Amish girl whose elders have impressed upon her
the importance of adhering to the simple ways of her people, is
horrified when one of her hen eggs hatches into an extremely fancy
bird.
    ISBN 0-553-05884-3 —ISBN 0-553-07062-2
    [1. Amish—Fiction. 2. Peacocks—Fiction. 3. Eggs—Fiction.]
I. Title.   89-27856
PZ7.P75186Ju 1990   CIP
[E]—dc20   AC

JUST PLAIN
FANCY

PATRICIA POLACCO

A BANTAM LITTLE ROOSTER BOOK
NEW YORK · TORONTO · LONDON · SYDNEY · AUCKLAND

Kaleb and his two daughters hurried along Lancaster County Road in their buggy. Cars whizzed by them, but they paid no mind. *Clop, clop, clop* went the horse's hooves on the pavement.

"Papa," Naomi asked, "why don't we have a car like the English?"

"It is not our way, child. We are in no hurry," he said as he drew up the reins and slowly directed the horse into their farmyard.

PENNSTA
HATCH
EXOTIC & DOMESTIC BIRDS

While their father unharnessed and watered the horse, Naomi and Ruth skipped toward the henhouse. The chickens were Naomi's responsibility. She saw to their feeding and watering as well as the collecting of their eggs.

"Everything around here is so plain," Naomi complained. "Our clothes are plain, our houses are plain, even our chickens are plain. It would pleasure me—just once—to have something fancy."

"Shaw, Nomi, you aughtn't to be saying such things," little Ruth scolded.

As Naomi and Ruth searched the field for eggs laid outside the henhouse, they spotted a very unusual one nestled in the tall grass down the drive and behind the henhouse, next to the road.

"This egg looks different from any I have ever seen," Naomi said quietly. "It's still warm—let's put it in Henny's nest. This one needs to be hatched." She gently picked up the egg and eased it into her basket.

Although it was a little bigger than Henny's other eggs and a little darker in color, Naomi gently tucked the egg into the nest while Henny and Ruth looked on.

"You're so good with chickens," Ruth chirped. "I just know you're going to get your white cap this year. Momma says you're ready."

Naomi was proud of her chickens and the way she raised them. The elders were coming for a working bee, or frolic, in the coming summer. And Naomi wondered whether her parents might present her with the white cap on that day. Her thoughts were interrupted by Ruth's voice.

"Ain't we pleasured," she said. "You wanted something fancy, and now you've got it."

As the days passed, Naomi and Ruth checked Henny's nest constantly. Every day they peered over the edge of the crib, watching for signs of cracks in the shells. Then, one day, the eggs hatched.

"Look at the little chick from the fancy egg, Nomi," Ruth squealed.

"That egg was fancy inside and out, wasn't it?" said Naomi. "Fancy. That's just what we'll name this chick."

"Fancy, Fancy, Fancy, Fancy," Ruth sang out as she jumped about. Naomi smiled and clapped her hands.

All that afternoon, the girls stayed with Henny, watching and studying their special little chick.

Weeks passed. Henny's chicks grew quickly and were soon scratching around in the dirt. They had all lost their yellow down feathers and had grown bright white ones. All of them, except Fancy. Fancy looked very different from the others. There was no doubt about it—this chick wasn't plain!

One afternoon in the washhouse, Naomi and Ruth overheard Aunt Sarai talking to cousin Hannah about a person in the neighboring Amish community.

"She dressed too fancy," Sarai said. "She had to be *shunned!*"

"Is it wrong to be fancy?" Naomi asked.

"Indeed, yes!" snapped Hannah. "We are plain folk. It is in our laws, the *Ordnung,* that we must be plain!"

"What does . . . 'shun' mean?" Ruth asked haltingly.

"Someone who is shunned is shamed in front of the elders. After that, friends and neighbors are instructed not to speak to that person. They are no longer one of us," Sarai answered with authority. Naomi and Ruth looked at each other and hurried outside to hang up the washing. Naomi felt botherment inside.

As soon as they were finished, the girls ran to the henhouse.

"What are we going to do?" Ruth asked. "Fancy is too fancy to be Amish!" Then Fancy ruffled up his feathers and did something that took their breath clean away.

"We'll have to hide him until we know what to do," Naomi said finally. "The elders will be here for the frolic tomorrow."

"He'll be shunned," Ruth whimpered. "Maybe we will be, too!"

They put Fancy into another part of the henhouse and locked the door.

The next morning, the neighboring Amish folk arrived for the frolic. The men and boys helped add a stable onto the Vleckes' barn. They worked hard in the sun while the womenfolk cooked and gossiped. Naomi and Ruth helped serve the food, pour lemonade, and thread needles for the women who were quilting. This should have been a happy day for them. But the girls were not pleasured because they were sad with worry about Fancy.

When she had served the last ladle of lemonade, Naomi started toward the henhouse. Just then she noticed the open door. But before she could get there to shut it, Fancy darted out and ran toward the gathering, flapping his wings.

"Oh, no!" Naomi called out. "This is all my fault. I wanted something fancy. I should have known better than to make that kind of wish!"

Tears ran down Ruth's cheeks when she saw what had happened. "Poooor Fancy," she cried. "Now he'll be shunned."

Over . . . Under . . . Around . . . Through. . . . Naomi ran after Fancy, trying to catch him before anyone noticed. And that's about the time that Fancy decided to head straight for the elders. He flew at Martha, the oldest member of the gathering. Adjusting her glasses, she gasped as he flew over her head just before landing on the clothesline where the quilts were airing.

"Please don't shun him," Naomi cried. "I did this! I made him fancy," she sobbed. At that moment, pleased with all the attention, Fancy ruffled his feathers and did for the guests what he had done for the girls in the henhouse the day before. Those who weren't speechless were stunned!

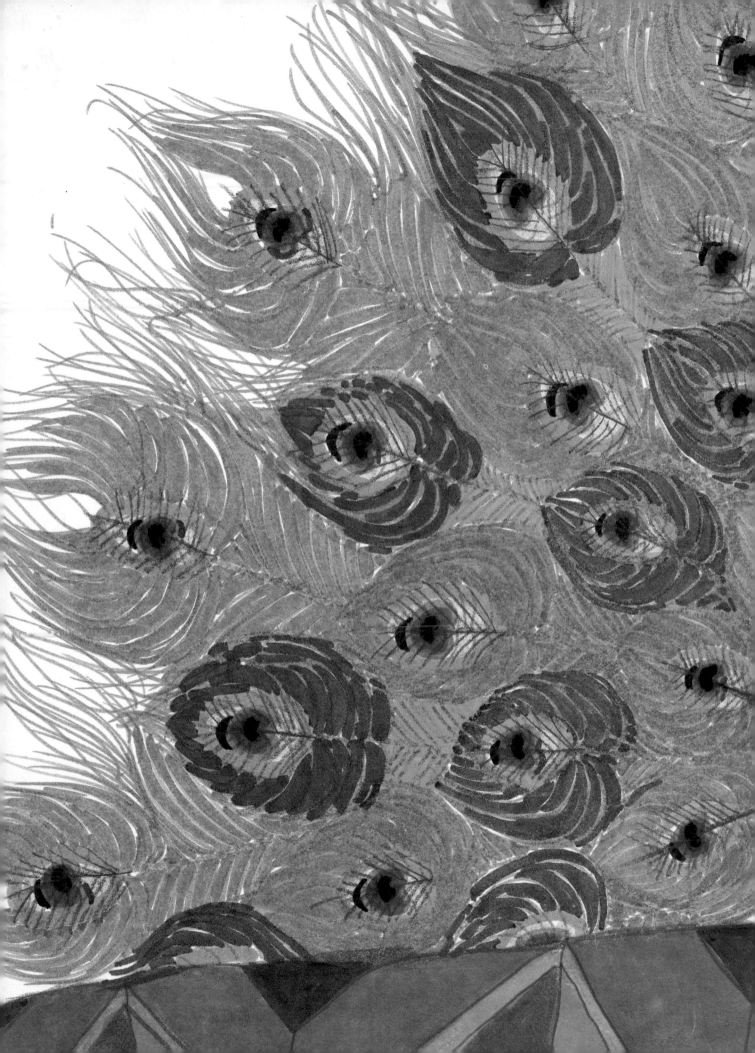

"Dry your tears, child." It was Martha who finally spoke. "This isn't your doing. This be God's handiwork. Only He could think up colors like that."

"You mean you aren't going to shun him?" Ruth asked.

"One can only be shunned for going against the ways of our people," Martha continued. "This is no plain old chicken. This be one of God's most beautiful creations. He is fancy, child, and that's the way of it."

All who were gathered there rejoiced in Fancy's beauty. "I believe you have this coming, child," old Martha said as she held out the new white organdy cap. Your family believes you have earned this well. And I agree. Not only have you given good and faithful care to your flock of chickens, but you have also raised one of the finest peacocks I ever did see!"

Standing proudly amidst the gathering, Naomi held Fancy in her arms. She had learned many things that day.

And although no one ever quite knew how Fancy came to be hatched by Henny, it was never questioned. Plainly it was a miracle . . . and sometimes miracles are JUST PLAIN FANCY!